As nice as PIE

Gary Sheppard & Tim Budgen

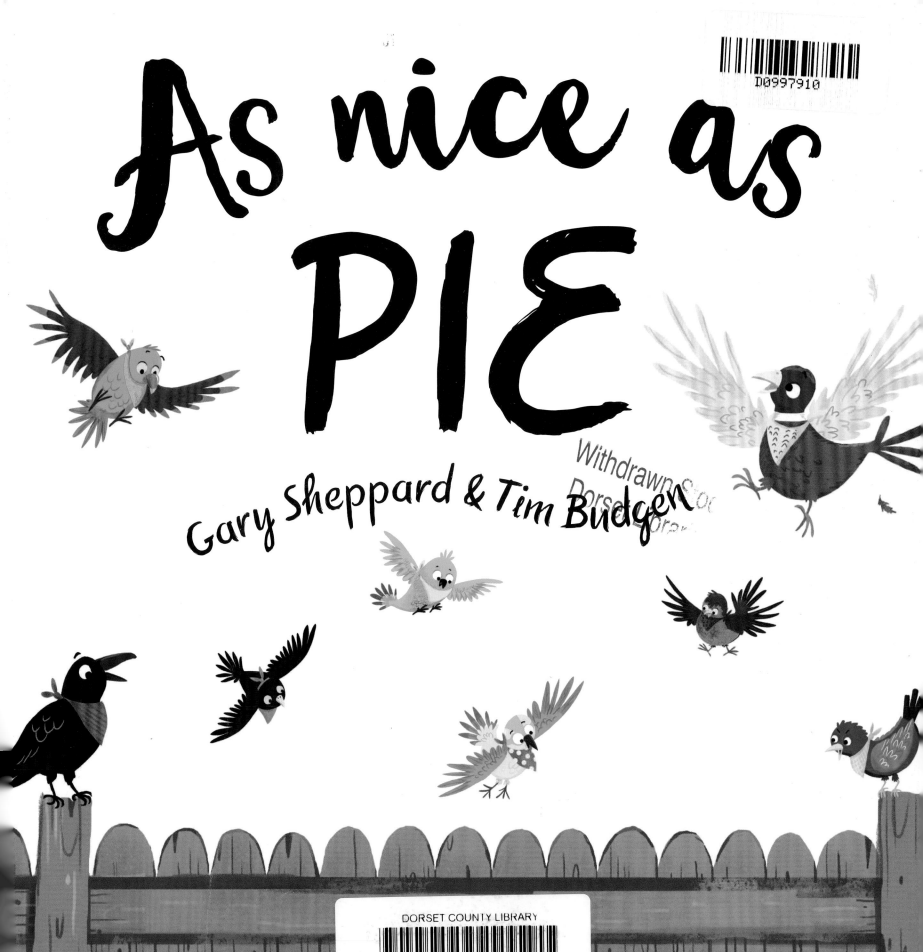

Mavis Manewaring was **kindly** and **caring**.
She loved nothing more than **cooking** and **sharing**.

One morning she saw a lone bird on her shed,
so she threw it a fistful of freshly baked bread.

Next day when she looked, the birds numbered **two**,
so she made them some biscuits and off they both flew.

The day after that, the birds totalled **three**,
so she baked up a batch of buns for their tea.

A week or so later, there must have been **twenty**...
...birds scoffing pastries and pasties aplenty!

In less than a month there were **hundreds**, perhaps,
with bellies all bulging from bacon in baps.

There were great greedy **gannets**, a plump **parakeet**,

some chubby-cheeked **crows**, all desperate to eat.

There were potbellied **pigeons**, a rather round **rook**,
impatiently waiting for Mavis to cook.

Each meal they would make
a most terrible row,

"BRING US OUR FOOD

AND BRING US IT NOW!"

"Stop!" Mavis shouted, "Can't you all wait?
Can't you all see I've a lot on my plate?!"

In all of a flap, she cooked up a plan,

as she crimped round the crust of a forty-foot flan.

She asked all the birds to cover their eyes,
"I've made you a dish called Birdie Surprise!"

"I just need the **filling** and then it's complete,
just stand over there and you're ready to **eat**!"

"Get on with our meal!" a dove rudely cooed,
"And what's the big secret inside of our food?"

"Good question!" said Mavis, "As that's the surprise.
It's YOU that's the filling inside of these pies!"

They opened their eyes. They were up to their knees, wading in gravy and freshly-picked peas.

"Let me out! Let me out!"
came the squawk from a parrot,
as it panicked and perched upon a raw carrot.

Mavis gave them a choice: "You can either be filling, or be **nice as pie** and show that you're willing, to help me to open the shop of my dream, and bake tasty pies as part of a team."

"So will you all help me? Is that a fair deal?
Or would you still rather be served as a meal?!"
"We'll do it!
We'll do it!" came the hasty replies,
"We'll happily help you to make tasty pies!"

They all worked together, from
pigeon to **pheasant**.

Stood feather to feather,
the birds were most pleasant.

The brown **speckled sparrows** plucked out the marrows.

The **woodpeckers** washed them and wheeled them in barrows.

The **chaffinches** chirped as they chopped up the veg.

The **ravens** rolled pastry, the **crows** crimped the edge.

Pie

The **starlings** made sure that the shop was all stocked, then the door was unlocked and the customers flocked.

The team's **tasty pies** all flew from the shelves, and they cheered with a feeling of **pride** in themselves.

The End

As Nice as Pie
An original concept by author Gary Sheppard
© Gary Sheppard

Illustrations by Tim Budgen
Tim is represented by Good Illustration
www.goodillustration.com

Published by MAVERICK ARTS PUBLISHING LTD
Studio 3a, City Business Centre, 6 Brighton Road,
Horsham, West Sussex, RH13 5BB +44 (0) 1403 256941
© Maverick Arts Publishing Limited November 2016

A CIP catalogue record for this book is available at the British Library.

ISBN: 978-1-84886-222-7

www.maverickbooks.co.uk